BLACK BEAUTY

ANNA SEWELL

Abridged and Simplified

1001 ÇİÇEK
kitaplar

BİNBİR ÇİÇEK KİTAPLAR
Yuva Mahallesi 3702. Sokak No: 4 Yenimahalle / Ankara
Tel:+90-312 396 01 11 Faks: +90-312 396 01 41
www.binbircicekkitaplar.com
Publisher Certificate No: 12382
Printing House Certificate No: 13651

ISBN: 978-605-341-278-6
ANKARA, 2015

Series Editor : A. Gazi Vural
Layout Design : Özlem Çiçek Öksüz
Cover Design : Mehmet Yaman
Printed in : Yorum Basın Yayın San. Ltd. Şti.
İvedik Organize Sanayi Bölgesi Matbaacılar Sitesi
35. Cadde, No: 36-38
06370 Yenimahalle – Ankara

Cover Design and Layout:
lodos
Business Design & Development

BİNBİR ÇİÇEK CLASSICS

Stage 1

1. The Jungle Book – *Rudyard Kipling*
2. Gulliver's Travels – *Jonathan Swift*
3. The Prince and the Pauper – *Mark Twain*
4. Alice in Wonderland – *Lewis Carroll*
5. The Wizard of Oz – *L. Frank Baum*
6. The Adventures of Tom Sawyer – *Mark Twain*

Stage 2

1. Heidi – *Johanna Spyri*
2. Around the World in Eighty Days – *Jules Verne*
3. Black Beauty – *Anna Sewell*
4. The Adventures of Pinocchio – *Carlo Collodi*

Stage 3

1. Robinson Crusoe – *Daniel Defoe*
2. Little Women – *Louisa M. Alcott*
3. Oliver Twist – *Charles Dickens*
4. Treasure Island – *Robert Louis Stevenson*

Stage 4

1. The Adventures of Huckleberry Finn – *Mark Twain*
2. Twenty Thousand Leagues Under the Sea – *Jules Verne*

Stage 5

1. The Count of Monte Cristo – *Alexandre Dumas*
2. Great Expectations – *Charles Dickens*

Stage 6

1. The Time Machine – *H. G. Wells*
2. Jane Eyre – *Charlotte Brontë*

About the Author

Anna Sewell (1820 – 1878) is well-known as **'the British author of the children's classic Black Beauty (1877).'** It is her only book. Sewell's concern for the humane treatment of horses began early in life when she spent many hours driving her father to and fro the station from where he left for his work. She was crippled at a young age, and though she had difficulty in walking, she could drive a horse-drawn carriage. Later, after reading an essay on animals by Horace Bushnell, she stated that one of her goals in writing was "to induce kindness, sympathy, and an understanding treatment of horses."

Sewell's introduction to writing began in her youth when she helped edit the works of her mother – a deeply religious, popular author of juvenile bestsellers. Sewell spent the last seven or eight years of her life—confined to her house as an invalid—writing *Black Beauty*. The book, a fictional autobiography of a gentle highbred horse, had a strong moral purpose and is said to have been instrumental in abolishing the cruel practice of using the checkrein.

Contents

1
MY EARLY HOME

The first place I remember was a large and pleasant meadow. It had a pond of clear water in it. On one side of the *meadow* was a *plowed* field. On the other side by the road stood our master's house. At the top of the meadow was a spread of fir plantation. At the bottom was a running *brook*.

When I was young, I could not eat grass. I lived upon my mother's milk. We used to stand by the pond when it was hot. We lived in our warm shed when it was cold. Our shed was near the plantation. At night, I lay down close by my mother.

As I grew old enough to eat grass, my mother went out to work in the daytime. She came back in the evening.

There were six young colts in the meadow besides me. We used to play together by galloping round and round the field. We often used to bite and kick each other during playtime.

One day, my mother instructed me to be a gentle horse. She said : 'The colts who live here are good colts but they have not learned manners. You come from a family of well-mannered horses. Your father has a great name in this area. Your grandfather won the cup at New Market races for two years. Your grandmother was the gentlest of all the horses. I think you have not even seen me kick or bite. I want you to grow up gentle. You should give up bad ways. You should never bite or kick even in play.'

I have always followed my mother's advice. She was wise and our master respected her very much. Her name was Duchess but he often called her Pet.

Our master was a kind man. He gave us good food and *lodging*. We were all fond of him. My mother used to neigh with joy when she saw him at the gate of his house. He used to ask my mother, 'How is your little Darkie?'

He called me Darkie, as I was black. He would give me a piece of bread, which was very good. He sometimes brought a carrot for my mother. I think we were his *favourite* horses.

The plowboy named Dick sometimes came into our field to pluck blackberries. After that, he would throw stones and sticks at us. This made us gallop. It was only fun for him but sometimes a stone would hit and hurt us.

One day, he was throwing stones at us and did not know that the master was in the next field. The master watched everything and then he caught Dick by the arm. He gave him a punch on the ear. Dick roared with pain and surprise. Our master gave him his due money and warned him never to come back on the farm again.

We never saw Dick anymore. Old Daniel, the man who looked after the horses, was as gentle as our master. So, we were well off.

2

THE HUNT

This *incident* happened before I was two years old. I and other colts were feeding at the lower part of the field. Soon, we heard something like a cry of dogs. The oldest of the colts said, 'There are the *hounds*!' Then, we all moved towards the upper part of the field. My mother was also standing nearby with an old riding horse. She seemed to know all about it and said, 'They have found a hare. They are hunting it. We shall see the hunt if they come this way.'

The dogs came tearing down the field of wheat next to ours. They did not bark. They only kept on a 'Yo! Yo, o, o! Yo, o, o!' at the top of their voices. After them came a number of men on horseback, galloping very fast. We also wanted to gallop with them. But they were soon away into the fields lower down. Just then, the dogs stopped barking. They ran about every way with their noses to the ground.

The old horse told me that both the men and the dogs were running after some hare for a hunt. But the dogs became quite as they had lost the scent. The huntsmen were still running after the hare.

Soon, the huntsmen were back at full speed. The dogs began shouting 'Yo ! Yo, o, o!' again. This time, they were coming straight towards our meadow where the high bank overhung the brook.

'Now we shall see the hare,' said my mother. Just then a hare rushed by. The dogs also came dashing across the field, followed by the huntsmen. The hare tried to get through the fence. But it was too late. The dogs were

Hunting hares

already upon her. We heard one shriek and that was the end of her. One of the huntsmen rode up and whipped off the dogs. Then, he held the hare up by the leg. All the gentlemen were pleased to see the hare torn and bleeding.

I was so *astonished*. There was a sad sight by the brook. Two fine horses were down. One was struggling in the stream, and the other was groaning on the grass. One of the riders was getting out of the water covered with mud, and the other lay quite still.

'His neck is broken,' said my mother.

'And serves him right, too,' said one of the colts.

I thought the same, but my mother did not join with us.

'Well! No,' she said, 'you must not say that; but though I am an old horse, and have seen and heard a great deal, I never yet could make out why men are so fond of this sport. They often hurt themselves and spoil good horses, and only for a hare or a fox.

We were listening to my mother. Many of the riders had gone to the young man; my master was the first to raise him. His head fell back and his arms hung down, and everyone looked very serious. They carried him to our master's house. I heard afterwards that it was young George Gordon, the squire's only son.

There was now riding off in all directions to the doctor's, to the farrier's, and no doubt to Squire Gordon's, to let him know about his son. When Mr. Bond, the *farrier*, came to look at the black horse, that lay *groaning* on the grass, he felt him all over, and shook his head. One of his legs was broken. Then someone ran to our master's house and came back with a gun; there was a loud bang and the black horse moved no more.

My mother seemed much troubled; she said she had known that horse for years, and his name was 'Rob Roy'; he was a good bold horse, and there was no vice in him. She never would go to that part of the field afterwards.

Not many days after, we heard the church bell *tolling* for a long time; looking over the gate we saw a long strange black coach that was covered with black cloth and was drawn by black horses. They were carrying young Gordon to the churchyard to bury him. He would never ride again. What they did with Rob Roy, I never knew. But it was all for one little hare.

3

MY BREAKING IN

I was now growing handsome; my coat had grown fine and soft, and was bright black. I had one white foot, and a pretty white star on my forehead. When I was four years old, Squire Gordon came to look at me. He seemed to like me, and said, 'When he has been well broken in, he will do very well.' My master said he would break me in himself, as he should not like me to be frightened or hurt. The next day he began.

Everyone may not know what breaking in is; therefore I will describe it. It means to teach a horse to wear a *saddle* and *bridle* and to carry on his back a person. Besides this, to have a cart or a chaise fixed behind him, so that he cannot walk without *dragging* it after him.

Now, I was to have a bit and a bridle. My master gave me some oats and after a good deal of *coaxing*, he got the bit into my mouth. The bridle was also fixed. It was a nasty thing. Next came the saddle. My master put it on my back very gently, while Old Daniel held my head. One morning, my master got on my back and rode me round the meadow on the soft grass. I felt strange but proud to carry my master. He continued and I became *accustomed* to it.

The next unpleasant business was putting on the iron shoes. The blacksmith took my feet in his hand and cut away some of the hoof. Then he took a piece of iron in the shape of my foot. He clapped it on with nails into my hoof. The shoe was firmly on.

Then, my master made me wear a stiff heavy collar on my neck and a bridle with great sidepieces against my eyes called blinkers. Next, there was a small saddle with a strap that went right under my tail. In time, I got used to everything.

4

BIRTWICK PARK

It was early in May. There came a man from Squire Gordon's. He took me away to the Hall. My master said, 'Good bye Darkie. Be a good horse. Always do your best to please your master.' I could not say 'Good bye,' so I put my nose into his hand. He patted me kindly, and I left my first home.

Squire Gordon's Park skirted the village of Birtwick. It was entered by a large iron gate, at which stood the first lodge. Then along a smooth road, there was another gate at which stood the other lodge. It brought to the gardens beyond which lay the home paddock, the orchard, and the stables.

The stable into which I was taken was very *roomy*. A large window that opened into the yard made it airy too. I was put into the loose box of the stable. It is a great thing to have a loose box because the horse in such a box is not tied up. He is left loose to do as he pleases. I was never in a better box than that. Even the walls were not very high. I could see all that went around me.

The groom gave me some very nice oats. He patted me and went away. When I had eaten my corn, I looked around. In the stall next to mine stood a little fat grey pony with a pretty head and a *pert* nose. I asked the pony, 'How do you do? What is your name?'

He turned and said, 'My name is Merrylegs. I am very handsome. I carry the young ladies on my back and our mistress in the low chair.

They admire me a lot, and so does James.'

Black Beauty with Merrylegs

'Are you going to live next door to me in the box?'

I said, 'Yes.'

'Well, then,' he said. 'I hope you are good tempered. I do not like anyone next door who bites.'

Just then a horse's head looked over from the stall beyond and spoke, 'So it is you who have turned me out of my box.'

'I beg your pardon,' I said, 'I have turned no one out. The man who brought me put me here and it is my wish to live at peace.'

'Well,' she said, 'I do not want to have words with a young thing like you.' I said no more.

In the afternoon when she went out, Merrylegs told me all about it. 'The thing is this,' Merrylegs said 'Ginger has a bad habit of biting and *snapping*. That is why they call her Ginger, and when she was in the loose box, she used to snap very much. One day she bit James in the arm and made it bleed. Miss Flora and Miss Jessie, who are fond of me, were afraid to come into the stable. They used to bring nice things to eat, an apple or a carrot, or a piece of bread, but after Ginger stood in that box they dare not come, and I missed them very much. I hope they will now come again, if you do not bite or snap.'

I told him I never bit anything but grass, hay, and corn, and could not think what pleasure Ginger got in it.

Merrylegs said, 'Well, I don't think she does find pleasure. It is just a bad habit. She says no one was ever kind to her, and why should she not bite? But I can tell you there is not a better place for a horse all round the country than this. John is the best *groom* that ever was. He has been here fourteen years. He is a very kind boy. It is all Ginger's own fault that she did not stay in that box.'

5

A FAIR START

The name of the coachman was John Manly. He had a wife and one little child. They lived in the coachman's cottage, which was near the stables.

The next morning he took me into the yard and gave me a good grooming. The Squire came in to look at me. He seemed pleased and said, 'John, I meant to have tried the new horse this morning, but I have other business. You may as well take him around after breakfast. That will show his *paces*.'

'I will, sir,' said John.

After breakfast he came and fitted me with a bridle. Then he brought the saddle, but it was not broad enough for my back. He saw it in a minute and brought another, which fitted nicely. He rode me first slowly, then a *trot*, then a *canter*, and when we were on the common he gave me a light touch with his whip, and we had a splendid gallop.

As we came back through the Park we met the Squire and Mrs. Gordon walking. They stopped, and John jumped off.

'Well, John, how does he go?'

'First-rate, sir,' answered John.

'That's well,' said the Squire. 'I will try him myself tomorrow.'

The next day I was brought up for my master. I found he was a very good rider, and thoughtful for the horse too. When he came home, the lady was at the hall door as he rode up.

Black Beauty with saddle on

'Well, my dear,' she said. 'How do you like him?'

'He is exactly what John said,' he replied. 'A very pleasant horse. What shall we call him?'

'He is really quite a beauty, and he has such a sweet face. What do you say to calling him Black Beauty?' she said.

'Black Beauty, yes, I think that is a very good name. It shall be his name,' and so it was.

When John went into the stable, he told James that master and mistress had chosen a good sensible English name for me. They both laughed and James said, 'If it was not bringing back the past, I should have named him Rob Roy, for I never saw two horses more alike.'

'That's no wonder.' Said John, 'Did you not know that Farmer Grey's old Duchess was the mother of them both?'

So poor Rob Roy who was killed at that hunt was my brother! I did not wonder that my mother was so troubled. It seems that horses have no relations; at least, they never know each other before they are sold.

John seemed very proud of me. He used to make my *mane* and tail almost as smooth as a lady's hair, and he would talk to me a great deal. I grew very fond of him. He was so gentle and kind.

James Howard, the stable boy, was as gentle and pleasant in his way, so I thought myself well-off.

A few days after this, I had to go out with Ginger in the carriage. I wondered how we should get on together. But everything was comfortable. Except laying her ears back when I was led up to her, she behaved very well. She did her work honestly, and did her full share, and I never wish to have a better partner in double harness. After we had been out two or three times together we grew quite friendly and sociable.

Our master had two other horses that stood in another stable. One was Justice, a *roan cob* for the luggage cart; the other was an old brown hunter, named Sir Oliver, who was past work by now because of age. He sometimes did a little light carting on the state, or carried one of the young ladies when they rode out with their father. He was very gentle and could be trusted with a child as well as Merrylegs.

I was quite happy in my new place. I had a little airy stable and the best of food. What more could I want? Why, liberty! For three years and a half of my life I had had all the liberty I could wish for.

Now, I must stand up in a stable night and day except when I am wanted, and then I must be just as steady and quiet as any old horse that has worked twenty years. Straps here and there, a bit in my mouth, and blinkers over my eyes!

I am not complaining. I only mean to say that for a young horse full of strength and spirits, it is hard never to have a bit more liberty to do, as you like.

Sometimes we had our liberty for a few hours. On Sundays in the summer time.

It was a great treat to be turned out into the Home Paddock. The grass was so cool and soft to our feet; the air so sweet, and the freedom to do as you liked was so pleasant; to gallop, to lie down, and roll on our backs, or to nibble the sweet grass.

6
GINGER

One day when Ginger and I were standing alone in the shade we had a talked a lot. She wanted to know all about my bringing up and breaking in, and I told her.

Soon, Ginger began to tell me that her story was a different one from mine. She said, 'I was taken from my mother when I was very young *weaned*, and put with a lot of other young colts; none of them cared for me. There was no kind master like yours to look after me.

A footpath ran through our field and very often the great boys passing through would *fling* stones to make us gallop. Sometimes we were hurt too and so we settled it in our minds that boys were our natural enemies.

Breaking in was also a bad time for me. Several men came to catch me. Then they applied all the force to set the bit, the saddle and so on. They held me so tight all the while that I could hardly draw my breath.

Then it was dreadful to be shut up in a stall day after day instead of having my liberty, and I *fretted* and *pined* and wanted to get loose.

There was no gentleness in my master named Samson. If I did not do what he wanted, he would make me run round with that long *rein* in the training field till he tired me out.

After some time, a dealer to match another chestnut horse bought me. For some weeks he drove us together, and then we were sold to a fashionable gentleman and were sent up to London. It was there when I was driven with the bearing rein. It is a dreadful thing. I like to toss my head about and hold it high myself but then, I was obliged to hold it there for hours, and that was a *torture.* Besides, I had two bits instead of one. So, I almost fretted at the bits and rein.'

Did not your master care for you? I said.

'No,' said she, 'he only cared to have a stylish turn out. As such we were reined even tighter. Instead of being kind, he made me suffer like anything. There was always the soreness in my mouth on account of the bit. In addition, there was also the pain in my neck because of the bearing rein, of course. I could not help it. I began to snap and kick. I soon broke a lot of harness and kicked myself clear; so that was the end of that place.

'After this, I was sent off to Tattersall's to be sold. Because of my handsome appearance, another dealer bought me. He tried me with different bits, and soon found out what I could bear. At last, he drove me quite without a bearing rein. He then sold me to a gentleman in the country. He was a good master. I was getting on very well. But soon, his old groom left him and a new one came. The man was as hard as Samson. If I did not move in the stall the moment he wanted me, he would hit me. Everything he did was rough, and I began to hate him. One day, I bit him. After that, he never dared to come into my stall again. He complained against me to the master and I was sold off again.

'It was then that I came here, after making up my mind that men were my natural enemies.'

Well, I said, I think it would be a real shame if you were to bite or kick John or James.

She said, 'I did bite James once, but John said, try her with kindness.'

Instead of punishing me, James came to me and stroked me gently. I was touched. I have never snapped at him since then.'

I was sorry for Ginger. However, I found that as the weeks went on, she grew much more gentle and cheerful. She improved day-by-day. Everybody noticed the change. Kindness was what she had wanted.

7
MERRYLEGS

Mr. Blomefield, the Vicar, had a large family of boys and girls. Sometimes, they used to come and play with Miss Jessie and Miss Flora. When they came, there was plenty of work for Merrylegs. Nothing pleased them so much as riding him all about the *orchard*.

One afternoon, he had been out with them a long time. Then James bought him in and said, 'There, you *rogue*, mind how you behave yourself.'

'What have you been doing Merrylegs?' I asked.

'Oh' said he, 'I have only been giving those young people a lesson. I just *pitched* them off backwards.'

'What?' said I, 'You threw the children off? Did you throw Miss Jessie or Miss Flora?'

He said, 'Of course not. I am as careful of the young ladies as the master could be. I am the best friend and the best riding master those children have. It is not they. It is the boys. These boys rode me by turns all around the orchard for a good hour. They had each cut a great hazel stick for a riding whip. They laid it on a little too hard. I stopped twice by way of a hint. The one who was *whipping* me could not understand. I just rose up on my hind legs and let him slip off behind. Then the other boy got up. As soon as he began to use his stick, I laid him on the grass, and so on, till they were able to understand, that was all.

'If I were you,' said Ginger, 'I would have given those boys a god kick, and that would have given them a lesson.'

Merrylegs said, 'I do not wish to anger our master or make James ashamed of me; besides, those children are under my charge when they are riding. I cannot be ungrateful to the kind treatment I have received here for five years. Above all, this is a good place, which is hard to find these days, if I took to kicking, I might be sold off. I might then find myself a slave under a *butcher's* boy, or worked to death at some seaside place where no one cared for me. I hope I shall never come to that.'

8

A TALK IN THE ORCHARD

Ginger and I had more of the racing blood in us. Our greatest pleasure was when we were saddled for a riding party, the master being on Ginger, the mistress on me, and the young ladies on Sir Oliver and Merrylegs.

I had often wondered how it was that Sir Oliver had a very short tail. One day I asked him by what accident it was that he had lost his tail. He said, 'It was no accident! It was a cruel act! When I was young I was taken to a place where these things were done. I was tied up. Then they came and cut off my long, beautiful tail.'

'How dreadful!' I exclaimed.

'Dreadful! Yes, it was. And not only because of the pain but that how could I ever brush the flies off my sides and my hind legs any more? I tell you it is a lifelong loss. But thank heaven, they don't do it now.'

'What did they do it for then?' said Ginger.

'For fashion!' said the old horse.

'I suppose it is fashion that makes them strap our heads up with those horrid bits in London,' said Ginger.

'Of course!' it is. Fashion is one of the wickedest things in the world. Now look, for instance, at the way they serve dogs. They cut off their tails to make them look *plucky*. They shear up their little ears to a point to make them look sharp. Why don't they cut their own children's ears into points to make them look sharp?'

Though Sir Oliver was gentle, yet what he said was all so new and dreadful to me. I found a bitter feeling towards men rise up in my mind. Ginger was too excited and declared that men were both *brutes* and *blockheads.*

'Who talks about blockheads?' said Merrylegs. 'I believe that is a bad word.'

'Bad words were made for bad things,' said Ginger.

Merrylegs said sadly, 'You know that master, and John, and James are always good to us. So talking about bad men in such a place as they have given us does not seem fair.'

This wise speech of Merrylegs cooled us all down.

To turn the subject I said, 'Can anyone tell me the use of blinkers?'

'No!' said Sir Oliver, 'because they are of no use.'

Justice said, 'They are used to prevent horses from getting so frightened as to cause accidents. They say that a horse would be so frightened to see the wheels of his own cart carriage coming behind him, that he would be sure to run away if blinkers were not used.'

Sir Oliver said, 'Blinkers are dangerous things in the night. We horses can see much better in the dark than men. Many an accident would never have happened if horses might have had the full use of their eyes.'

Merrylegs said, 'I believe John does not *approve* of blinkers; I heard him talking with master about it one day. John said it would be a good thing if all colts were broken in without blinkers. So let us cheer up and have a run to the other side of the orchard. The wind has blown down some apples.'

So we broke off our conversation to *munch* some very sweet apples, which lay *scattered* on the grass.

9

A STORMY DAY

Once, my master had a long journey to go on business. I was put into the *dogcart*. I always liked to go in the dogcart. John also went with the master. It was raining very much.

In one part of the road, the water was up to my knees. The meadows were under this water. But the master drove gently. So, it did not matter.

We got to the town. The master's business engaged him a long time. So, I had to wait. Late in the afternoon, we started for home. The wind was blowing fast. We had never been out in such a storm.

We were going along the *skirts* of a wood. The branches were swaying above us. We were afraid of the branches that could fall down upon us anytime.

All of a sudden, there was a crashing sound. An oak tree was torn up by the roots and had fallen just before us. I was frightened. We could not move forward anymore.

John *advised* that we could go back to the four crossways to find the other way. He said, 'It will make us late but the horse is fresh.'

So, we went back. We found the other way over the bridge. But I felt there was something wrong as soon as my feet touched the bridge. I dared not go ahead. I stopped.

Both my master and John asked me to move on but I did not. I knew very well that the bridge was not safe.

Just then, a man on the other side of the bridge ran out of his house. He tossed a torch at us and shouted, 'The bridge is broken in the middle. If you come on, you will fall into the river.'

My master took a sigh of *relief*. John gently led me towards the right hand road by the riverside. The wind was calmer than before. I trotted quietly on the soft roads.

At last, we came to the Park gates, The mistress was anxiously waiting for us. She asked the master, 'Are you really safe, my dear?'

The master replied, 'If your Black Beauty had not been wiser than us, we whould all have been carried down the river.'

John then led me to the stable and gave me a good supper. I was glad.

10

THE DEVIL'S TRADEMARK

One day, John and I had been out on some business of our master's. When we were returning on a long straight road, we saw a boy trying to leap a pony over a gate. The pony would not take the leap. The boy whipped him, but the pony turned off. Then the boy gave him a hard trashing. He *knocked down* and hit the pony.

When we were nearly at the spot, the pony threw up his heels and sent the boy into a thorny *hedge*. Then the little pony galloped towards his home. John laughed aloud as the boy struggled among the thorns.

The boy asked for help. John answered, 'I think you are quite in the right place. A little scratching will teach you not to leap a pony over a gate.'

Then, John rode off. We turned off the right because we wanted to go to farmer Bushby's house. Soon we came within the sight of the house. The farmer was looking very frightened.

Mr. Bushby asked us, 'Have you seen my boy? He went out an hour before on my black pony, and the creature has just come back without the rider.'

John told him the whole story. The boy's mother began to cry when she heard that her son, Bill, was in trouble. But the farmer did not let her go to meet his son in the hedge. He said, 'Bill wants a lesson. I shall see that he gets it. It is not the first time he has ill-used a pony.'

After that, the farmer thanked us. So we went on. John told James the entire story as we reached home. James said, 'Serves him right. I knew that boy at school. He used to catch flies and pull off their wings. One day, I saw him and gave him a box on the ears. He roared in such a style that the boys and the master ran in to see who was murdered. I showed the master the poor flies. The master punished him. He asked him to stand on the stool for the whole afternoon.'

After that, the master talked to us about cruelty. He said, 'Cruelty is the devil's *trademark*. Only love is God's mark.

John agreed and said, 'Yes, there is no religion without love.'

11
JAMES HOWARD

One morning early in December, John had just led me into my box after my daily exercise. He was strapping my cloth on. James was coming in with some oats. The master came into the stable. He looked serious. He held an open letter in his hand.

'Good Morning, John,' said the master. 'I want to know if you have any complaints to make of James?'

'Complaint, sir? No, sir.'

'Is he *industrious* at work and respectful to you?'

'Yes sir, always.'

'That's well; but I must put another question. Have you any reason to *suspect* that when he goes out with the horses, he stops to go into the houses where he has no business, leaving the horses outside?'

'No, sir! Certainly not! I can trust his word and I can trust his work.'

The master said, 'James, my lad, set down the oats and come here. I have a letter from my brother-in-law, Sir Clifford Williams, of Clifford Hall. He wants me to find him a *trustworthy* young groom. His old coachman, who has lived with him thirty years, is getting *feeble*, and he wants a man to work with him and get into his ways. When the old man will be pensioned off, you could get the place. It would be a good start for you. Think it over and let me know what you wish.'

In a few days after this conversation, it was settled that James should go to the Clifford Hall. In the meantime, he was to get all the practice in driving that could be given to him.

12

THE FIRE

Later on in the evening, a traveller's horse was brought in by the second ostler. While he was cleaning him, a young man with a pipe in his mouth walked into the stable to gossip.

'I say, Towler,' said the hostler, 'Just run up the ladder into the *loft* and put some hay down into this horse's rack. But first lay down your pipe.'

'All right,' said the other, and went up to put down the hay. James came in to look at us and then the door was locked.

I cannot say how long I had slept but I woke up very uncomfortable. The air seemed all thick and choking. I heard Ginger coughing. The other horses too moved about *restlessly*. The stable was full of smoke. All the horses were fully awake by now. Some were pulling at thin *halters*, others were stamping.

At last I heard steps outside. The Ostler who had put up the traveller's horse began to untie the horses. He was trying to lead them out but he seemed so frightened that he frightened me still more. The first horse would not go with him. The second would also not stir as he was tried, and so would the third one. He came to me next. Of course that was of no use. He tried us all by turns and then he left the stable, a failure.

No doubt, we were foolish. Danger seemed to be all around. As I looked upward through the bars of my empty rack, I saw a red light flickering on the wall. Then I heard the cry of 'Fire' outside. The old Hostler quietly and quickly came in.

He got one horse out, and went to another. The flames were playing round the trap door. The next thing I heard was James' voice. It said, 'Come on, my beauties. It is time for us to be off. So wake up and come along.'

I stood nearest the door. So, he came to me first. He then led me out of the stable. The next moment I gave a loud joyful neigh, for I saw James coming through the smoke leading Ginger with him. We were moving towards the marketplace. There came a sound of galloping feet and loud rumbling wheels.

'It is the fire engine! The fire engine!' shouted two or three voices, 'Stand back, make way!'

Two horses dashed in with the heavy engine behind them. The fireman leaped to the ground. We got out as fast as we could into the broad quiet marketplace. Master led the way to a large hotel on the other side. There was a dreadful sound before we got into our stalls. The shrieks of those poor horses that were left burning to death in the stable were terrible.

At first no one could guess how the fire had been caused. At last, a man said he saw Dick Towler go into the stable with a pipe in his mouth. When he came out, he had not one with him!

Then the Ostler said he had asked Dick to go up the ladder to put down some hay, but had told him to lay down his pipe first. Dick denied taking the pipe with him, but no one believed him. I remember our John Manly's rule, never to allow a pipe in the stable. It ought to be the rule everywhere.

The rest of our journey was very easy. After sunset we reached the house of our master's friend. We stopped two or three days at this place and then returned home. We were glad to be in our own stable again. John was equally glad to see us.

Before he and James left us for the night, James said, 'I wonder who is coming in my place.'

'Little Joe Green at the Lodge,' said John.

'Little Joe Green! Why? He is a child!'

'Yes, he is only fourteen and a half but he is quick and willing. I know the master would like to give him a chance. So, I have agreed to try him for six weeks.'

The next day Joe came to the stables to learn all he could before James left. He learned to sweep the stable, to bring in the straw and hay etc. He was a nice little bright fellow, and always came whistling to his work.

At last the day came when James had to leave us. He looked quite *downhearted* that morning. So, John cheered him up but everyone was sorry to lose James.

13
GOING FOR THE DOCTOR

One night, I was lying down in my straw fast asleep. The stable bell ringing very loud suddenly awaked me. I heard the door of John's house open, and his feet running up to the hall. He unlocked the stable door and came in. He then called me out, 'Wake up, Beauty!'

Almost before I could think, he had got the saddle on my back and the bridle on my head. He just ran round for his coat and then took me at a quick trot up to the Hall door. The Squire stood there with a lamp in his hand.

'Now, John,' he said, 'Ride for your mistress' life; there is not a moment to lose. Give this note to Doctor White. Give your horse a rest at the inn. Be back as soon as you can.'

John said, 'Yes, sir,' and started for the job. He said to me, 'Now, Beauty, do your best,' and so I did. My old grandfather who won the race at New Market could not have gone faster.

When we came to the bridge, John *patted* my neck. 'Well done, Beauty! Good old fellow,' he said. After an eight miles run, we came to the town. The church clock struck three as we drew up at Doctor White's door.

John rang the bell twice, and then knocked at the door like thunder. A window was thrown open. Doctor White in his nightcap said, 'What do you want?'

'Mrs. Gordon is very ill, sir. Master wants you to go at once. He thinks she will die if you cannot get there. Here is a note.'

'Wait,' he said, 'I will come.' Then he shut the window, and was soon at the door. He was willing to help but he was stuck in a problem. He said, 'My horse has been out all day and is quite done up. Can I take your horse?'

'He has come at a gallop nearly all the way, sir, and I was to give him a rest here; but I think my master would not be against letting you have my horse if that could save a life. If you think it will be fit, you can have my horse.'

'All right,' he exclaimed, 'I will soon be ready.' Saying this, he went in. He soon came out with his riding whip.

'You need not take that, sir. Black Beauty will go till he drops. Take care of him, sir, if you can. I should not like any harm to come to him.'

The Doctor agreed. And within a minute we had left John far behind, The Doctor was a heavier man than John, and was not a good rider. However, I did my very best. When we came to the hill, the Doctor drew me up. 'Now, my good fellow, take some breath,' he said to me.

I was glad. Breathing helped me on, and soon we were in the Park. Joe was at the lodge gate. My master was at the Hall door. He had heard us coming. The Doctor went into the house with him. Joe finally led me to the stable.

I was happy to be back home. But I was so tired that I could only stand and pant. I steamed all over-like a pot on fire. Poor Joe! He was young and small and still he did the very best he knew. He rubbed my legs and my chest. But he did not put my warm cloth on me as he thought I was so hot that I should not like it. Then he gave me a pail full of water to drink. He also gave me some hay and some corn afterwards. Thinking he had done everything right, he went away. Soon I began to shake and tremble. I wished for my warm thick cloth. I wished for John, but he had eight miles to walk. So I lay down in my straw and tried to go to sleep.

After a long while, I heard John at the door. I gave a low *moan*, for I was in great pain. He came by my side in a moment. He covered me up with two or three warm cloths and then ran to the house for some hot water. He made me some warm *gruel*, which I drank. Then I think I went to sleep.

John seemed to be very much put out. I heard him say to himself, over and over again, 'Stupid boy! Stupid boy! No cloth put on, and I dare say the water was cold too; boys are not good.' But Joe was a good boy after all.

I was now very ill. A strong swelling had attacked my lungs. I could not draw my breath without pain. John nursed me day and night.

'My poor Beauty,' he said one day, 'my good horse, you saved your mistress' life!'

I was more *delighted* to have heard the good news than to have heard the word of praise for me.

14

ONLY IGNORANCE

I do not know how long I was ill. Mr. Bond, the horse doctor, came everyday. One day, he bled me. John held a *pail* for the blood. I felt very faint after it. I thought I would die!

Ginger and Merrylegs had been moved into the other stable, so that I might be quiet. The fever had made me very quick of hearing. Any little noise seemed like a shout.

One night, John had to give me some medicine. Thomas Green came in to help him. After I had taken it, John said he should stay half an hour to see how the medicine settled. Thomas said he would stay with him. So they went and sat down on a bench that had been brought into Merrylegs' stall.

For a while both men sat silent, and then Tom Green said in a low voice : 'I wish, John, you'd say a bit of a kind word to Joe; the boy is quite broken-hearted. He says he knows it was his entire fault but he did not mean the harm. He also says that if Beauty dies, no one will ever speak to him again.

After a short pause, John said slowly, 'You must not be too hard upon me, Tom. I know he meant no harm. I know he is a good boy. If you think I am hard on the boy, I will try to give him a good word tomorrow, that is, I mean if Beauty is better.'

'Well, John! Thank you. I knew you did not wish to be too hard, and I am glad to see it was only *ignorance*.'

John's voice almost startled me as he answered, 'Only ignorance! How can you talk about only ignorance so lightly? Do not you know that it is the worst thing in the world, next to *wickedness*?

I heard no more of this conversation, for the medicine did well and sent me to sleep. In the morning, I felt much better.

15
THE PARTING

I had now lived in this happy place three years, but sad changes were about to come over us. We heard from time to time that our mistress was ill. Then we heard that she must leave her home at once and go out to a warm country for two or three years. Everybody was sorry.

The master began to make arrangements for leaving England. The first of the party who went were Miss Jessie and Flora with their governess. They came to bid us goodbye. Then we heard what had been arranged for us. Master had sold Ginger and me to his old friend, the Earl of W–, for he thought it to be a good place for us. Merrylegs was given to the Vicar on the condition that he should never be sold. Joe was engaged to take care of him. John had the offer of several good places, but he said he should wait a little and look round.

The evening before they left, the master came into the stable to give his horses the last pat. He seemed very *low-spirited*.

'Have you decided what to do, John?' he said, 'I find you have not accepted any of those offers. If in any way I can help you, write to me.'

Master gave John the name and address, and then he thanked him for his long and faithful service. John said, 'You and my dear mistress have done so much for me that I could never repay it. But we shall never forget you, sir,' Then, Master gave John his hand and they both left the stable.

The last sad day had come. The footman and the heavy luggage had gone off the day before. Only master and mistress and her maid were left. Ginger and I brought the carriage up to the Hall for them. Master came down the steps carrying the mistress in his arms. He placed her carefully in the carriage. The house servants stood round crying.

'Goodbye again! We shall not forget any of you,' and he got in saying, 'Drive on, John.'

When we reached the railway station, I heard the mistress saying in her own sweet voice, 'Goodbye, John, God bless you.'

John made no answer. Perhaps he could not speak. Poor Joe! He stood close up to our heads to hide his tears. Very soon the train came *puffing* up in the station. Then, after two or three minutes, the guard whistled and the train *glided* away.

When it was quite out of sight, John came back. 'We shall never see her again,' he said, 'never.' He took the reins, *mounted* the box, and then Joe drove slowly home. But it was not our home now.

16
EARLSHALL

The next morning after breakfast, Joe put Merrylegs into the mistress's low chaise to take him to the vicarage. Merrylegs neighed to us from the yard. Then John put the saddle on Ginger and the leading rein on me, and rode us across the country about fifteen miles to Earlshall Park, where the Earl of W– lived. He was a fine looking middle aged man. His voice said that he expected to be obeyed. He called a groom to take us to our boxes, and invited John to take some *refreshment.*

We were taken to a light, airy stable, and placed in boxes *adjoining* each other. In about half an hour, John and Mr. York, who was to be our new *coachman*, came in to see us.

'Now, Mr. Manly,' he said, 'I can see no fault in these horses, but I should like to know if there is anything particular in either of these that you would like to mention.'

'Well,' said John, 'I don't believe there is a better pair of horses in the country. The black one has the most perfect *temper* I ever knew. I suppose he has never known a hard word or a blow since he was foaled. But the chestnut I fancy must have had bad treatment. She came to us snappish, but when she found what sort of a place ours was, it all went off by degrees. If she is treated well, there is not a better and more willing animal than she is.

'Of course,' said York, 'I quite understand.'

Just as they were going out of the stable, John stopped and said, 'I had better mention that we have never used the 'bearing rein' with either of them.'

'Well,' said York, 'if they come here they must wear the bearing rein. I prefer a lose rein myself but my lady will have style. If her carriage horses were not reined uptight, she would not look at them.

'I am sorry for it. Very sorry!' said John, 'But I must go now, or I shall lose the train.' He then came round to each of us to pat and speak to us for the last time. His voice sounded very sad.

The next day, Lord W— came to look at us. He seemed pleased with our appearance.

In the afternoon, we were harnessed and put in the carriage. As the stable clock struck three, we were led round to the front of the house. We heard the rustling sound of silk as my lady came down the flight of stone steps. She stepped around to look at us. She did not seem pleased about something, but she said nothing and got into the carriage. This was the first time I was wearing a bearing rein. It certainly was a *nuisance* not to be able to get my head down now and then. I felt anxious about Ginger.

The next day at three o'clock, we were again at the door. We heard the silk dress rustle. The lady came down the steps and said, 'York, you must put those horses' heads higher; they are not fit to be seen.'

York got down and said very respectfully, 'I beg you pardon, my lady, but these horses have not been reined up for three years. It would be safer to bring them to it by degrees, but if your ladyship pleases, I can take them up a little more.'

'Do so,' she said.

That day we had a steep hill to go up. I wanted to put my head forward and take the carriage up. But all the strain came on my back and my legs. When we came in, Ginger said, 'If they strain me up tight, why, let them look out! I can't bear it and I won't.'

Day-by-day, hole, by hole, our bearing reins were shortened. I began to dread it. Ginger too seemed restless. At last, I thought the worst was over. For several days, there was no more shortening. I was determined to make the best of it and do my duty.

17

A STRIKE FOR LIBERTY

One day, my lady came down and said, 'Drive to the Duchess of B–.' s.' Then she added, 'Are you never going to get those horses' heads up, York? Raise them at once.'

York came to me first. He fixed the rein so tight that it was almost intolerable. Then he went to Ginger. The moment York took the rein, Ginger took her *opportunity* and *reared* up so suddenly that York had his nose roughly hit, and his hat knocked off. She went on *plunging*, rearing and kicking in a most *desperate* manner. At last, she kicked right over the carriage pole, after giving me a severe blow. York sat himself down flat on her head to prevent her struggling, at the same time calling out, 'Unbuckle the black horse!'

The groom soon set me free from Ginger and the carriage, and led me to my box. He just turned me in as I was and ran back to York. I stood angry. My head still strained up. I was very miserable.

Before long, however, Ginger was led in by two grooms, a good deal knocked about and bruised. York came with her and gave his orders, and then came to look at me. He felt me all over, and soon found the place above my *hock* where I had been kicked. It was swollen and painful. He ordered it to be sponged with hot water.

Lord W– was much put out when he learned what had happened. He blamed York for giving way to his mistress. Ginger was never put into the carriage again. I was obliged still to go in the carriage, and had a fresh partner called

"Unbackle the Black Horse!" shouted York.

Max. He had always been used to the tight rein. I asked him how it was he bore it.

'Well,' he said, 'I bear it because I must, but it is shortening my life.'

'I can't say,' he replied, 'but the dealers and the horse doctors know it very well.

What I suffered with that rein for four long months in my lady's carriage would be hard to describe. Before that, I never knew what it was to foam at the mouth, but now the action of the sharp bit on my tongue caused me to foam. Besides this, there was a pressure on my windpipe, which often made my breathing very uncomfortable. When I returned from my work, my neck and chest were strained and painful. I felt worn and depressed.

In my old home, John and my master were my friends; but here, I had no friend. York might have known, and very likely did know, how that rein harassed me. But he took it as a matter that could not be helped. Nothing was done to relieve me.

18

REUBEN SMITH

Reuben Smith was in charge of the stables when York went to London. He was gentle and very clever in his management of horses. Everybody liked him. He had only one great fault. That was the love of drink.

It was now early in April. The family was expected home in May. Colonel Blantyre was obliged to return to his *regiment*. It was arranged that Smith should drive him to the town and ride back. For this purpose, I was chosen for the journey. At the station, the Colonel put some money into Smith's hand and bade him good-bye. He said, 'Take care of your young mistress and keep Black Auster only for the lady.'

Smith rode me to the White Lion, and ordered the hostler to feed me well and have me ready for him at four o'clock. A nail in one of my front shoe had moved from its position as I came along. The hostler did not notice it till just about four o'clock. Smith did not come into the yard till five, and then he said he should not leave till six, as he had met with some old friends. The man then told him of the nail. But Smith took no heed and said, 'That will be all right till we get home.'

He did not come at six but nine o'clock. He called for me in a loud rough voice. He seemed in a very bad temper. He was giving me a sharp cut with his whip. I was going at full speed. The roads were stony. My shoe became looser. Soon, it came off. Smith was in fact, too madly drunk to notice anything. I was forced to gallop at my utmost speed and my shoeless foot suffered dreadfully.

This could not go on. The pain was too great. I stumbled and fell with violence on both my knees. Smith was flung off by my fall. I could see him lying a few yards beyond me. He made one slight effort to rise but he could not. He was *groaning* heavily. I could do nothing for him as I was suffering with an intense pain in both my feet and my knees myself.

I tried to listen for some sound of a horse, or wheels, or footsteps for help. But at this time of the night, there were no sounds except a few low notes of a nightingale. I listened hard for quite a long while. After sometime, I heard the sound of a horse's feet. The road to Earlshall led through plantations that belonged to the Earl. The sound came in that direction. I hoped it might be someone coming in search of us. As the sound came nearer, I could *distinguish* Ginger's steps. I was overjoyed to hear an answering neigh from Ginger, and several men's voices too.

The men stooped down over Smith and raised him up. There was no life in him as could be seen. They laid him down again and came to look at me. They soon saw my cut knees. They exclaimed wishfully, 'Only if Smith was in his right senses!' Then, a handkerchief was bound round my wound and I was led home.

At last, I reached my box. The horse doctor saw me in the morning. The best was done to make a good cure. It was a long and painful one. I was healed after all, but I did not lose the scars on my knees. Tough luck!

Smith's death had been sudden and an unexpected one. The landlord and hostler at the White Lion gave evidence that he was *intoxicated* when he started from the inn. The case was quite plain. I was cleared of all blame.

As soon as my knees were sufficiently *healed*, I was turned into a small meadow for a month or two. No other creature was there. I felt very lonely. One morning the gate opened and dear old Ginger was slipped off her halter and left in the meadow. She was brought to be with me. We had pleasure in each other's company. We passed our time together till the family returned from the town.

One day the Earl came into the meadow. He examined us carefully. He noticed the scar on my knees and then decided that I must be sold. Through the *recommendation* of York, the master of livery stables bought me.

19

DRIVERS OF A JOB-HORSE

My new master kept a good many horses and carriages of different kinds for hire. So, in this place I was to get my experience of all kinds of bad and ignorant driving. Being a 'job-horse' here, I was let out to all sorts of people who wished to hire me.

First, there were tight-rein drivers. They seemed to think that all depended on holding the reins as hard as they could. Just such drivers have made some horses hard and insensible.

Then there are loose-rein drivers, who let the reins lie easily on our necks. Such gentlemen have no control over a horse, if anything happens suddenly. If a horse shies, or starts, or stumbles, they are nowhere and cannot help the horse or themselves, till the damage is done. Of course, such drivers are disliked by most of the horses as one would surely like to know that one's driver has not gone to sleep.

Then there is steam engine style of driving. These drivers were mostly people from towns. They never had a horse of their own and generally travelled by rail. They always seemed to think that a horse was something like a steam engine. They think that if only they pay for it, a horse is bound to go just as fast as they please. This steam engine style of driving wears us up faster than any other kind.

One spring, Rory (the horse that mostly went with me when a pair was ordered) and I had been out for the day. We had our own driver, and as he was always *considerate* and gentle with us, we had a pleasant day. We were coming home about twilight. Our road turned sharp to the left. As we neared the corner, I heard a horse and two wheels coming rapidly down the hill towards us. I could see nothing, but the next moment we were upon each other. Happily for me, I was on the side next the hedge. Rory was on the right side of the pole. The whole shock thus came upon Rory. His flesh was torn and he was bleeding. They said if it had been a little more to one side it would have killed him. The wound healed up after a period but *unfortunately*, Rory was *disabled*. As it was, he was ultimately sold off for coal carting. And that is a hard job where horses are required to move up and down the *steep* hills with heavy loads. I was sorry for Rory.

After the incident, I went in the carriage with a mare named Peggy. She had a very odd and slow pace. It was very unpleasant for any horse that pulled with her. But she was much liked by some ladies, because she was so gentle. She was soon sold to two ladies who drove themselves, and wanted a good, safe horse.

After she left us, another horse came in her stead. He was young, and had a bad name for shying and starting. I asked him what made him shy. He said, 'I was *timid* when I was young and was a good deal frightened to start on my own. So, my master always gave me whipping, which of course made me start on but this made me all the more frightened. I was never given a chance to understand that there was nothing to be frightened of. I am sure if my master had treated my habit of nervousness with patience, I would not have become as shy as I am now.'

I knew what my companion said was true. I wished that every young horse had as good a master as Farmer Grey and Squire Gordon.

20

A THIEF

One morning, I was put into a light *gig*, and taken to a house in Pulteney Street. Two gentlemen came out. The taller of them came round to my head. This gentleman took a great liking to me. So, he asked my master to sell me to a friend of his, who wanted a safe horse for riding. And so it came to pass that in summer I was sold to Mr. Barry.

My new master lived at Bath, and was much engaged in business. He engaged a man named Filcher as groom. My master knew very little about horses but he ordered *plenty* of good food for me. My groom also understood his business well and he groomed me *thoroughly*. I felt cared for; and so I thought myself to be well-off in this place.

Then things *gradually* changed. After a while I had only less than a quarter of oats I should have got. This began to tell upon my strength. However, I could not complain, nor make known my wants. I wondered my master did not see that something was the matter.

One afternoon, he rode out into the country to see a friend of his. This gentleman had a very quick eye for horses. He said, casting his eye over me, 'It seems to me, Barry, that your horse does not look as well as he did when you first had him.'

'Yes, I believe so,' said my master.

'How do you feed him?' he asked.

My master told him all that he ordered for me since I was bought. The other shook his head slowly, and began to feel me over.

After that, he hinted my master that there are often some mean people, wicked enough to rob a dumb beast of his food. He *suggested* that the matter must be looked into.

If could have spoken I could have told my master where his oats went to. My groom used to come every morning about six o'clock, and with him a little boy, who always had a covered basket with him. He used to go with his father into the harness room where the corn was kept. I could see them fill a little bag with oats out of the bin and be off.

Five or six mornings after this, just as the boy had left the stable, a policeman walked in, holding the child tight by the arm. Another policeman followed and asked him, 'Show me the place where your father keeps his rabbits' food.' There was no escape. He led the way to the corn-bin. Here the policeman found nothing but another empty bag. It was just like the bag which was found full of oats in the boy's basket. So the case explained itself quite clearly. The food meant for a horse was stolen for a rabbit's meal!

Filcher was cleaning my feet at the time when they took him off to the 'lock-up', and his boy with him, I heard afterwards was not held to be guilty, but the man was sentenced to prison for two months.

21

A HUMBUG

In a few days, my new groom came named Alfred Smirk. He was very *civil* to me, and never used me ill. He considered himself very handsome. He spent a great deal of time before a little looking glass in the harness room. When his master was speaking to him it was always, 'Yes, sir. Yes, sir.' I should say he was the laziest fellow I ever came near. Of course, it was a great thing not to be ill used, but then a horse wants something more than that.

One day, his master came in and said, 'Alfred, the stable smells rather strong. Should not you give that stall a good scrub, and throw down plenty of water?'

'Well, sir,' he said, 'I will do so if you please, sir, but it is rather dangerous, sir, throwing down water in the horse's box. The horses are very *apt* to take cold, sir.'

'Well,' said the master, 'I should not like him to take cold, but I don't like the smell of this stable. Do you think the drains are all right?'

'There may be something wrong, sir.'

'Then send for the bricklayer and have it seen to.'

'Yes, sir! I will.'

The bricklayer came and found nothing *amiss*. He charged the master five shillings, and the smell in my box was as bad as ever. But that was not all. Standing as I did on a quality of moist straw, my feet grew unhealthy and tender.

Now the fact was that hardly ever did he exercise me.

One day my feet were so tender that trotting over some fresh stones with my master on my back, I made two serious stumbles. He stopped at the farrier's and asked him to see me. The farrier said, 'This is the sort of thing we find in foul stables where the litter is never properly cleared out. If you will send him here tomorrow I will attend to the hoof.'

The next day I had my feet thoroughly cleansed and soaked in some strong *lotion*. The farrier ordered all the litter to be taken out of my box day-by-day, and the floor kept very clean. Then I was to have bran mashes, and not so much corn, till my feet were well again.

With this treatment, I soon regained my spirits. But Mr. Barry was so much disgusted at being twice *deceived* by his grooms that he decided to give up keeping a horse. I was, therefore, sold again.

My new master took my halter, and led me to an inn. He gave me a good feed of oats and stood by while I ate it, talking to his own self and talking to me. Half an hour after, we were on our way to London. So, I made up my mind for another new experience.

My new master was Jerry Barker. I never knew a better man than my new master. He was kind and good tempered and fond of singing. With his wife Polly, and children Harry and Dolly, they made a family of four merry people. Overall, it was a happy place for me.

22

THE GOLDEN RULE

On Sunday morning Jerry was cleaning me in the yard when Polly stepped up to him, looking very full of something.

'What is it?' said Jerry.

'Well, my dear,' she said, 'poor Dinah Brown has just informed that her mother is dangerously ill. She must go immediately if she wishes to see her alive. The place is more than ten miles away. If she takes the train, she would still have four miles to walk with the baby only four weeks old. That would be impossible. She wants to know if you would take her in your cab.'

'We will see about that. The horses are tired and I am tired too; and that is where it *pinches*.'

Polly said, 'You know, we should do to others as we should like they should do to us.'

'Polly, you sound as good as the minister. You may go and tell Dinah that I will be ready for her as the clock strikes ten. Now, just step round to the butcher Braydon's, and ask him if he would lend me his light *trap*. It would make a wonderful difference to the horse.'

She went and soon returned, saying that he could have the trap. I was *selected* for the journey, and at ten o'clock we started. It was a fine day, luckily.

Dinah's family lived in a small farmhouse. As we reached near the place, we could see two cows feeding in it. A young man asked Jerry to bring his trap into the meadow, and he would tie me up in the cowshed.

'If your cows would not be offended,' said Jerry.

The young man invited him for dinner in that hour. He wanted to thank Jerry for his kindness to Dinah.

Jerry thanked him for the invitation, but politely turned it down by saying that he had already got some dinner with him. Then he said that instead of dinner, he should definitely like to walk about in the meadow.

When my harness was taken off, I did not know what I should do first, whether to eat the grass, or roll over my back, or have a gallop across the meadow. I did all by turns. Jerry seemed to be as happy as I was. He sang. He picked flowers and tied them up. He also gave me a good feed of oats. But the time seemed all too short. I had never been in a field since I left poor Ginger at Earlshall.

Then we came home gently, and Jerry's first words were, 'Well, Polly, I have not lost my Sunday after all.' Then he handed Dolly the flowers and she jumped about for joy.

23

A SUCCESSOR FOR OLD CAPTAIN

Captain and I were great friends. I never thought that he would have to leave his home and go down the hill, but his turn came.

This is how it happened. I was not there, but I heard all about it. He and Jerry had taken a party to the great railway station over London Bridge. As they were coming back, Jerry saw a *brewer's* empty dray coming along somewhere between the Bridge and the Monument; it was being drawn by two powerful horses. The *drayman* was lashing his horses with his heavy whip. The dray was light and they started off at a *furious* rate. The man had no control over them. One young girl was knocked down and run over. And the next moment, they dashed up against our cab!

Jerry was thrown, but only bruised. Nobody could tell how he escaped the danger and it seemed like a miracle. Poor Captain got up very much cut and knocked about. He could hardly walk at that moment and therefore, Jerry led him home gently. The drayman was proved to be very drunk, and was fined. The brewer had to pay the damages to our master. But there was none who could pay damages to poor Captain.

Captain was a very old horse, and it was only Jerry's care that had kept him going at the cab-work so long. The farrier said he might mend up enough to sell for a few pounds, and that too, for no other work but *carting*. Jerry was very much put out to know that Captain had lost his *efficiency* for the cab-work. He considered something and said, 'No! A few pounds got by selling a good old horse into hard work and *misery* would be a cruel thing to do.' He thought the kindest thing he could do for the fine old fellow would be to put a sure bullet through his heart, and then he would never suffer more. The day after this was decided, Harry took me to the forge for some new shoes. When I returned, Captain was gone.

Jerry had now to look out for another horse. He soon heard of one through an *acquaintance*. He was a valuable young horse, but he had run away, smashed into another carriage, and so cut and blemished that he was no longer fit for a gentleman's stables.

'I can do with high spirits,' said Jerry, 'if a horse is not hard mouthed.'

'There is not a bit of vice in him,' said the man, 'his mouth too is very tender.'

'Likely enough! I will come and see him,' said Jerry.

The next day, Hotspur – that was his name – came home. He was a fine, brown horse and only five years old. I gave him a friendly greeting. Jerry patted and talked to him a great deal. Very soon, they understood each other.

Jerry said that with an easy bit, and plenty of work, he would be as gentle as a lamb. In fact, he settled in well, and Jerry liked him very much.

24

JERRY'S NEW YEAR

Christmas and the New Year are very merry times for some people. But for cabmen and cabmen's horses it is no holiday. There are so many parties that work is hard and often late. Sometimes driver and horse have to wait for hours while the merry people within are dancing away to the music.

We had a great deal of late work in the Christmas week, and Jerry's cough was bad. On the evening of the New Year, we had to take two gentlemen to a house in one of the West End Squares. We set them down at nine o'clock and were told to come again at eleven. 'But,' said one of them, 'as it is a card party, you may have to wait a few minutes, but don't be late.'

As the clock struck eleven we were at the door. The clock struck twelve, but the door did not open. The wind had been very cold and there was no shelter. At half-past twelve, Jerry rang the bell and asked the servant if he would be wanted that night. The reply said that we were wanted of course, and that we must wait for a short while.

At quarter past one the door opened, and the two gentlemen came out. They got into the cab and told Jerry where to drive. The place was nearly two miles. My legs were *numb* with cold, and I thought I should have stumbled. When the men got out, they never said they were sorry to have kept us waiting so long. Moreover, they were angry at the charge. However, Jerry never charged a penny more or less than what was his *due* and so they had to pay for the two hours and a quarter waiting.

At last, we got home. Jerry could hardly speak and his cough was dreadful. It was late the next morning before anyone came, and then it was only Harry. He cleaned us and fed us. He was very still, and neither whistled nor sang.

At noon he came again, and gave us our food and water. This time Dolly came with him. I could gather from what they said that Jerry was dangerously ill.

Two days passed but we only saw Harry and sometimes Dolly. On the third day, while Harry was in the stable, Government Grant came in.

'I would not go to the house, my boy,' he said, 'but I want to know how is your father.'

'He is very bad,' said Harry, 'he can't be much worse. They call it *bronchitis*.'

'That's bad, very bad,' said Grant, 'I know two men who died of that last week, but while there is life there is hope.'

'Yes,' said Harry quickly, 'and the doctor said that father had a better chance than most men, because he did not drink. I believe he will get over it.'

The Governor said, 'I am sure he will, my boy. He is the best man I know. I will look in early tomorrow.'

Early next morning he was there.

'Well?' said he.

'Father is better,' said Harry. 'Mother hopes he will get over it.'

'Thank God!' said the Governor, 'and now you must keep him warm. Jack (as they called me) will be all the better for the rest of the week or two in a warm stable. But this young one. Hotspur, will soon be all up on end if he does not get out. Now look here, will you tell your mother that if she is agreeable, I will come for him everyday to take him for a god spell of work. Whatever he earns, I will bring your mother half of it. That will help him with the horses feed. I will come at noon and hear what she says'.

At noon, I think he went and saw Polly, for he and Harry came to the stable together, harnessed Hotspur and took him out.

For a week or more he came for Hotspur. He said it was all good luck for him.

Jerry grew better but the doctor said that he must never go back to the cab work again. One afternoon Hotspur was brought in very wet and dirty.

While Harry was sponging off the mud from Hotspur's body and legs, Dolly came in, looking very full of something.

'Who lives at Fairstove, Harry? Mother has got a letter from there. And she seemed so glad that she ran upstairs to father with it.'

'Don't you know? It is the name of Mrs. Fowler's place. She is our mother's old mistress. Mother wrote to her last week about father giving up the cab-work. I wonder what she answers back. Run in and see, Dolly.'

In a few minutes Dolly came dancing to the stable.

'Oh! Harry, Mrs. Fowler says we are all to go and live near her. Her coachman is going away in the spring, and then she will want father in his place.

'That's good. It will suit father and mother both.'

It was quickly settled that as soon as Jerry was well enough, they should move to the country, and that the cab and horses should be sold as soon as possible.

This was heavy news for me. Since I left Birtwick I had never been so happy as with my dear master. Grant said at once that he would take Hotspur. The Governor promised to find a place for me where I should be comfortable.

The day came for going away. The family came to bid me good-bye. They stroked me a great deal with affection. Then finally, I was led to my new place.

25

JAKES AND THE LADY

I was sold to a corn dealer and baker, whom Jerry knew. If my master had always been on the premises, I do not think I should have been overloaded, but there was a foreman who was always hurrying and ordering something else to be taken on when I had quite a full load. My carter, whose name was Jakes, often said it was more than enough, but the other always *overruled* him.

Jakes, like the other carters, always had the bearing rein up. I found the work telling very much on my strength.

One day, I was loaded more than usual, I used all my strength, but I could not get on. This did not please my driver, and he laid his whip on badly. He was flogging me cruelly when a lady stepped quickly up to him, and said in a sweet voice, 'Oh! Pray do not whip your good horse any more; I am sure he is doing all he can, and the road is very steep, I am sure he is doing his best.'

'He must do something more than his best. That's all I know, madam,' said Jakes.

'But is it not a very heavy load?' she said.

'Yes, yes, too heavy,' he said, 'but that is not my fault. The *foreman* came just as we were starting, and ordered more of weight to be put on.'

'You see,' she said, 'you do not give him a fair chance. He cannot use all his power with his head held back as it is with that bearing rein. If you would do better.'

'Well, well,' said Jakes, 'anything to please a lady of course. How far would you wish it down, madam?'

'Quite down, give him his head altogether.'

"That was a real lady. I'll be bound for it," said Jakes

The rein was taken off. What a comfort it was! I tossed it up and down several times to get the aching stiffness out of my neck.

Jakes took the rein. The load moved on, and I pulled it steadily.

The lady had walked along the footpath. She stroked and patted my neck.

'You see he was quite willing when you gave him the chance. You won't put that rein on again, will you?'

'Well, ma'am, I can't deny that having his head has helped him up the hill, but if he went without a bearing rein I should be the laughing stock of all the carters; it is the fashion, you see.'

'We have no right to distress any of God's creatures without a very good reasons; I thank you for trying my plan with your good horse, and I am sure you will find it far better than the whip. Good- day,' she stepped across the path, and I saw her no more.

'That was a real lady, I'll be bound for it,' said Jakes. I must do him the justice to say that he let my rein out several holes, but the heavy loads went on. No horse can stand against overloadig. I was getting so pulled down from this cause that a younger horse was bought in my place. Besides, I had a badly lighted stable. The *depressing* effect weakened my sight; the *glare* of sunlight was very painful to my eyes. Several times I stumbled over the *threshold.*

However, as there was no permanent injury to my sight, I was sold to a large cab owner.

26

HARD TIMES

I shall never forget my new master. His name was Nicholas Skinner. Skinner had a low set of cabs and a low set of drivers; he was hard on men, and the men were hard on the horses. In this place we had no Sunday rest even it was in the heat of summer. I had never known the utter misery of a cab-horse's life before I came here.

My life was *utterly* miserable. One day I went on the stand at eight in the morning. Soon our cab was called for. There was a party of four:a noisy, *blustering* man with a lady, a little boy, and a young girl. Box after box was dragged up and lodged on the top of the cab.

The load was heavy, I had had neither food nor rest since the morning, and I did my best till we came to Ludgate Hill. Then my feet slipped from under me, and I fell heavily to the ground. I had no power to move, and I thought now I was going to die. Someone came and loosened the throat strap of my bridle. Someone said, 'He's dead, he'll never get up again.' Some cold water was thrown over my head. I found my life coming back, and a kind voiced man was patting me and *encouraging* me to rise. After some more attempts, I was gently led to stables, which were nearby. Here some warm gruel was brought to me, which I drank thankfully.

In the evening I was sufficiently recovered to be led back to Skinner's stables. In the morning Skinner came with a farrier to look at me. He said, 'This is a case of

"He's dead, he'll never get up again!"

overwork more than disease; there is not an ounce of strength in him.'

'Then he must go to the dogs,' said Skinner, 'I have no meadows to nurse sick horses.'

The farrier said, 'There is a sale of horses coming off in about ten days. If you rest him and feed him up, he may pick up, and you may get more than his skin is worth, at any rate.'

Upon this advice, Skinner, rather unwillingly, gave orders that I should be well-fed and cared for. The stableman carried out the orders with a much better will. Ten days of perfect rest and plenty of good food improved my condition. When the twelfth day after the accident came, I was taken to the sale.

27

A FARMER AND HIS GRANDSON

At this sale, I found myself in the company with the old, broken-down horses.

I noticed a man who looked like a gentleman farmer, with a young boy by his side. When he came up to my companions and me, he gave a pitiful look round upon us. I saw his eye rest upon me.

The man who had brought me for sale now put in his word, 'This horse is just pulled down with overwork in the cabs; he's not an old one. The veterinary said that a six months' run-off would set him right up. Let him have a chance.'

The little boy looked very excited.

The farmer slowly felt my legs, which were much swelled and strained; then he looked at my mouth.

'What is the lowest you will take for him?' said the farmer.

'Five pounds, sir,'

And so I was finally sold off. The boy could hardly control his delight, and the old gentleman seemed to enjoy his pleasure.

Mr. Thoroughgood, my new master, gave orders that I should have hay and oats every night and morning. 'You, Willie,' said he, 'must take care of him; I give him in charge to you.'

The boy was proud of his charge. He always came with kind words and *caresses*. I grew very *fond of* him. He called me Old Crony. Sometimes he brought his grandfather who always looked closely at me,

The perfect rest, the good food, the soft *turf* and gentle exercises soon began to tell on my condition and my spirits. During winter my legs improved so much that I began to feel quite young again.

'He's growing young, Willie; we must give him a little gentle work now.'

'Oh! Grandpapa, how glad I am you bought him!'

'We must now be looking out for place for him, where he will be valued.' said the *former*.

28

MY LAST HOME

One day the groom cleaned and dressed me with such extraordinary care that I thought some new change must be at hand. Willie seemed half anxious, half merry, as he got into the chaise with his grandfather.

At the distance of a mile or two from the village, we came to a pretty house. Willie rang the bell and asked if Miss Blomefield, or Miss Ellen, was at home. Yes, they were. So, while Willie stayed with me, Mr. Thoroughgood went into the house. In about ten minutes, he returned, followed by two ladies; one tall, pale lady, *wrapped* in a white shawl, *leaned on* a younger lady, with dark eyes and a merry face; the other, a very *stately* looking person was Miss Blomefield. The younger lady was Miss Ellen. She said that she liked me and that I had such a good face. The tall, pale lady said that she should always be nervous in riding behind a horse that had once been down, as I might come down again, and if I did, she should never get over the fright.

Mr. Thoroughgood announced, 'I do not want to influence you. If you feel *inclined*, you can have him on trial and then decide.'

It was then arranged that I should be sent for the next day.

In the morning, a smart looking young man came for me. At first he looked pleased, but when he saw my knees, he said in the *disappointed* voice, 'I did not think you would have recommended my ladies a blemished horse like that, sir.'

'Handsome is – that handsome does,' said my master. 'You are only taking him on trial. If he is not as safe as any horse you ever drove, send him back.'

I was led home, placed in a comfortable stable, fed and left to myself. The next day, when my groom was cleaning my face, he said, 'That is just like the star that Black Beauty had!' He then began to look me over carefully.

'White star in the forehead, one white foot on the off side, this little knot just in that place. It must be Black Beauty! Why, Beauty! Beauty! Do you know me? Little Joe Green that almost killed you?' said he and began patting and patting me as if he was quite overjoyed.

I could not say that I remembered him, for now he was a fine-grown young fellow, but I was sure he was Joe Green. I put my nose up to him, and tried to say that we were friends.

In the afternoon Miss Ellen was going to try me, and Green went with her. I soon found that she was a good driver. She seemed pleased with my paces. I heard Joe telling her about me, and that he was sure I was Squire Gordon's old Black Beauty.

When we returned, the other sisters came out to hear how I had behaved myself. She told them what she had just heard, and said, 'I shall certainly write to Mrs. Gordon, and tell her that her *favourite* horse has come to us. How pleased she will be!'

After this it was quite decided to keep me and call me by my old name of "Black Beauty".

I have now lived in this happy place a whole year Joe is the best and kindest of grooms. My work is easy and pleasant. I feel my strength and spirits are coming back again.

My troubles are all over. I fancy I am still in the orchard at Birtwick, standing with my old friends under the apple trees.

❀❀❀❀❀❀❀

VOCABULARY

Chapter 1

meadow : grassland
plowed : land prepared for plantation
brook : a fresh water stream
lodging : place for living.
favourite : a thing or person you like most

Chapter 2

incident : happening, event
hounds : hunting dogs
astonished : surprised
farrier : smith who shoes horses
groaning : crying out in pain
tolling : ringing of bells in a measured way

Chapter 3

saddle : seat used by a rider on the back of an animal
bridle : straps fitted to a horse's head for controlling the reins and the bit
dragging : pulling
coaxing : to persuade by fondling
accustomed : used to

Chapter 4

roomy : spacious
pert : rude

snapping	:	behaving impatiently in anger
groom	:	attendant of the horses

Chapter 5

paces	:	steps, rate of speed
trot	:	jog
canter	:	running speed
mane	:	long hair on the neck of a horse or lion
roan	:	having a double coloured coat
cob	:	strong horse with short legs

Chapter 6

weaned	:	taken off mother's milk
fling	:	throw
fretted	:	complained
pined	:	longed
rein	:	straps to control a horse
torture	:	suffering

Chapter 7

orchard	:	a garden of fruits
rogue	:	rascal
pitched	:	threw
whipping	:	striking forcefully
butcher	:	meat dealer

Chapter 8

plucky	:	courageous
brutes	:	cruel people

blockheads	:	fools
approve	:	give a favourable opinion
munch	:	chew thoroughly
scattered	:	lying here and there

Chapter 9

dogcart	:	two wheeled carriage drawn by a horse
skirts	:	edges, periphery
advised	:	suggested
relief	:	comfort

Chapter 10

knocked down	:	struck down
hedge	:	close-set row of bushes
trademark	:	symbol

Chapter 11

industrious	:	hard working
suspect	:	doubt
trustworthy	:	loyal, faithful
feeble	:	weak

Chapter 12

loft	:	room over a stable
restlessly	:	uneasily
halters	:	straps over the head of the horse
downhearted	:	sad, depressed

Chapter 13

patted	:	touch lightly in appreciation
moan	:	cry of pain

gruel	:	thin porridge
delighted	:	pleased

Chapter 14

pail	:	bucket
ignorance	:	lack of knowledge
wickedness	:	ill-conduct, harmful behaviour

Chapter 15

low-spirited	:	dull and sad
puffing	:	movement of a train while giving out smoke
glided	:	move smoothly
mounted	:	climbed into the seat.

Chapter 16

refreshment	:	light meal
adjoining	:	next, attached to
coachman	:	driver of the carriage
temper	:	nature
nuisance	:	a bother, troublesome

Chapter 17

opportunity	:	advantage or fair chance
reared up	:	rising up on hind legs
plunging	:	sudden forward movement
desperate	:	anxious
hock	:	joint in the hind leg of the horse

Chapter 18

regiment	:	orderly group of an army
groaning	:	crying in pain

distinguish	:	clearly identify
intoxicated	:	drunk
healed	:	repaired
recommendation	:	favourable suggestion

Chapter 19

considerate	:	kind
unfortunately	:	unluckily
disabled	:	incapable of normal functioning
steep	:	rising or descending with great inclination
timid	:	shy

Chapter 20

gig	:	a light two-wheeled carriage
plenty	:	lots, more than needed
thoroughly	:	completely and properly
gradually	:	slowly
suggested	:	advised

Chapter 21

civil	:	courteous
apt	:	suitable
amiss	:	out of place
lotion	:	liquid medicine or medication liquid
deceived	:	cheated

Chapter 22

pinches	:	hurts
trap	:	two-wheeled carriage
selected	:	chosen

Chapter 23

brewer	:	one who makes beer
drayman	:	driver of a large horse-drawn cart without fixed sides
furious	:	angry
carting	:	carrying load
efficiency	:	ability to work well
misery	:	suffering
acquaintance	:	a person known to one.

Chapter 24

numb	:	loss of sensation
due	:	owed as settled for services rendered
bronchitis	:	inflamation of the membrane of the airways of the lungs

Chapter 25

overruled	:	dominated and changed the decision
foreman	:	man in charge of a group of workers
depressing	:	sad
glare	:	angry stare
threshold	:	edge or the starting point

Chapter 26

utterly	:	to the extreme point
blustering	:	threatening
encouraging	:	giving hope

Chapter 27

caresses	:	touch lovingly
fond of	:	like strongly

turf	:	thick layer of grass
former	:	previous

Chapter 28

wrapped	:	covered
leaned on	:	used support
stately	:	grand
inclined	:	feel positively
dissappointed	:	unhappy
favourive	:	someone or something most liked

QUESTIONS ON TEXT

Chapter 1

1. What were the instructions given to Black Beauty by his mother?
2. Describe Black Beauty's early home.
3. How did the master at this place treat Black Beauty?
4. Who was Dick? How did he treat the horses.
5. What punishment did the master give to Dick?

Chapter 2

1. Describe the hunt.
2. What was the impression of the hunt on Black Beauty?
3. How did the hunt end?
4. What happened to the black horse?

Chapter 3

1. What is 'breaking in' for a horse?
2. Describe how Black Beauty was broken in.
3. How did Black Beauty feel about her 'breaking in' process?

Chapter 4

1. Describe Squire Gordon's home at Birtwick Park.
2. What kind of a stable did Black Beauty get here?
3. Who was Merrylegs? How did he feel about himself?
4. Why was Ginger named so?
5. Why did Merrylegs like John, their groom?

Chapter 5

1. How did the coachman John Manly treat Black Beauty?

2. Who named Black Beauty so and why?
3. What did Black Beauty find out about Rob Roy?
4. Who was Black Beauty's partner in double harness? How did the team work go?
5. Describe the other two horses in the stable.
6. What kind of life did Black Beauty have here?

Chapter 6

1. Why was Ginger a difficult horse?
2. Describe Ginger's 'breaking in'.
3. How did Samson, Ginger's new master, treat her?
4. Why did the new master not care for the horse's comfort?
5. Why did Ginger feel that men were her natural enemies?
6. How did Black Beauty feel for Ginger after hearing her story?

Chapter 7

1. Why did James have to tell Merrylegs to behave himself?
2. Why did Merrylegs behave badly?
3. How did Ginger feel about the incident that had made Merrylegs behave badly?
4. Why did Merrylegs not want to anger his master?
5. What did Merrylegs fear?

Chapter 8

1. What did Ginger and Black Beauty enjoy most? Why?
2. Why did Sir Oliver's tail worry Black Beauty?
3. Describe the problems Sir Oliver faced because of his short tail.

4. What did Sir Oliver say that made Black Beauty have a bitter opinion of men?
5. How did Merrylegs cool them down?
6. What is the use of blinkers?

Chapter 9

1. Why did Black Beauty and his master have to take the bridge for returning home?
2. Why was Black Beauty not ready to cross the bridge?
3. What did the man on the other side of the bridge call out?
4. How did the master and mistress feel about Black Beauty?

Chapter 10

1. Why did the boy whip the pony?
2. What did the pony do after being whipped?
3. What did John say to the boy?
4. How did the boy's father and mother feel about the incident?
5. What did James tell them about the boy's school life?

Chapter 11

1. Why did the Squire want to find out about James Worth as a groom?
2. Why did Sir Clifford want to change his groom?

Chapter 12

1. Why did Black Beauty wake up feeling uncomfortable?
2. Why were the horses not ready to go out with the ostler?
3. How had the stable caught fire?
4. Describe how the firemen put out the fire.

5. Why was the master ready to try the fourteen year old Joe Green?

Chapter 13

1. Why did Black Beauty have to ride one night?
2. What was the doctor's problem?
3. Why did John not allow the doctor to carry a whip?
4. How did Joe treat him when he reached home?
5. Why did Black Beauty begin to shake and tremble?
6. Even though Black Beauty was ill, what made him happy?

Chapter 14

1. How did the doctor treat Black Beauty?
2. What was John's reaction to the folly of Joe?
3. What was Tom's advice to John?
4. How did John react to the advice?

Chapter 15

1. Why had Black Beauty's master decided to move to a warm country?
2. To whom were Black Beauty and Ginger sold?
3. Describe John's feelings at the time of parting.

Chapter 16

1. On their arrival at Earlshall, what did the new owner ask Mr. Manly?
2. What was Mr. Manly's reply?
3. Why was John so sad on leaving the horses?
4. Describe the feelings of Black Beauty and Ginger when they were reined up?

Chapter 17

1. How did Ginger behave one day when she was reined in more tightly?

2. How did Lord W–, their new master, feel about the incident?
3. Describe Black Beauty's injury and the treatment given.
4. What kind of life did Black Beauty have here?

Chapter 18

1. Who was Reuben Smith? What kind of a man was he?
2. What happened one night in April when Smith came late?
3. What was he told by the ostler about Black Beauty's shoe?
4. How did Reuben Smith behave?
5. Describe the accident.
6. What was the effect of the accident on Black Beauty?
7. What happened to Black Beauty after her wounds had healed?

Chapter 19

1. Describe Black Beauty's life at the livery stables.
2. What is the difference between tight rein and loose reign?
3. What is the 'steam engine' style of driving?
4. How was Rosy hurt?
5. Why had the new horse become shy?

Chapter 20

1. Why was Black Beauty sold to Mr. Barry?
2. Who was Black Beauty's groom and how did he treat him?
3. What change took place gradually?

4. How did the change effect Black Beauty?
5. What did his master's friend tell him about Black Beauty's condition?
6. What was happening to Black Beauty's share of oats?
7. How was the theft discovered?
8. What punishment was given to the groom?

Chapter 21

1. How did the new groom Alfred Smith behave?
2. What went wrong with Black Beauty's stable?
3. How did the foul condition affect Black Beauty's health?
4. What treatment was given to Black Beauty?
5. Why was Black Beauty sold again?
6. Who was the new master? What kind of a man was he?

Chapter 22

1. What did Polly request Jerry to do? Why?
2. What was Jerry's response?
3. Why did Jerry turn down the dinner invitation?
4. What did Jerry want to do instead?
5. How did Black Beauty feel when his harness was taken off? What did he do?
6. What did Jerry do before returning to his home?

Chapter 23

1. How was the drayman driving his cart?
2. Describe the accident and its result.
3. What do you learn about Captain from this chapter?
4. Do you agree to the way Captain's miseries were put an end to?
5. Describe the new horse that replaced Captain.

6. How had Jerry come to know about him?
7. How did the new horse fit in with them?

Chapter 24

1. What makes Black Beauty say that Christmas and New Year are no holiday times for horses?
2. What happened on one New Year eve?
3. How did it effect Black Beauty and his master, Jerry?
4. Describe Jerry's illness.
5. Why did Jerry have a better chance of recovery than most men?
6. What did the governor decide about Black Beauty and Hotspur?
7. Where was Jerry going with his family?
8. How did Black Beauty feel on hearing this news?

Chapter 25

1. What did Black Beauty's new master do? How did it affect Black Beauty?
2. How did Jakes treat Black Beauty?
3. How did a lady help Black Beauty one day?
4. Did Jakes obey the lady? Why?
5. How did Black Beauty behave when they were taken off?
6. What did the lady teach him about behaving with all God's creatures?
7. Why did Black Beauty develop weak eyesight?

Chapter 26

1. How did the new master, Nicholas Skinner ruin his business?
2. Why does Black Beauty say that his life here was utterly miserable?
3. Describe the accident at Ludgate Hill.

4. What was the farrier's comment?
5. What was the advice of the farrier?

Chapter 27

1. Who bought Black Beauty at the sale?
2. What reason did the man have for buying a horse?
3. How did young Willie care for Black Beauty? What was he named here?

Chapter 28

1. Where did Willie and his father take Black Beauty?
2. Describe Miss Blomfield?
3. Why did Miss Ellen like Black beauty?
4. What was Miss Ellen alfraid of?
5. Describe Black Beauty's new stable and the groom's behaviour.
6. How did Black Beauty get back his name?
7. What was the surprise that awaited Black Beauty?
8. Describe the appearance of the new groom.
9. 'All's well that ends well!' How far do you think that this statement stands true with regard to Black Beauty's life?
10. What are your feelings for horses at the end of the story?

OTHER TITLES IN THE SERIES

STAGE 1

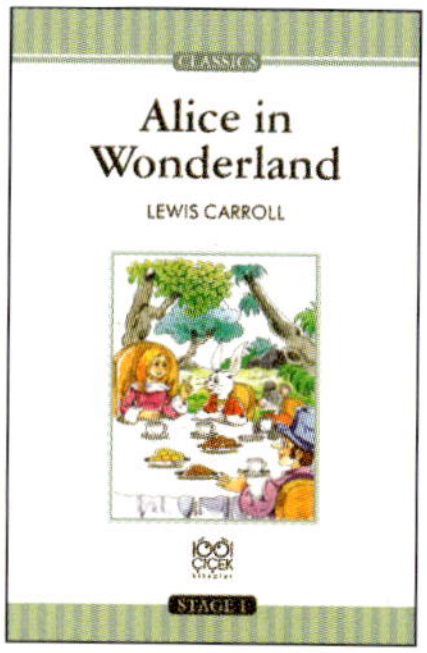

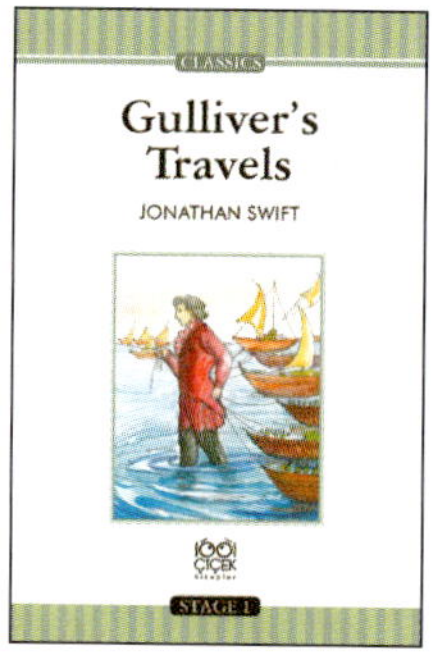

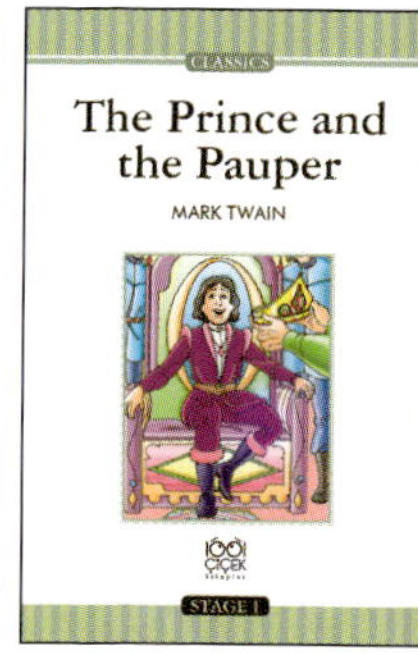

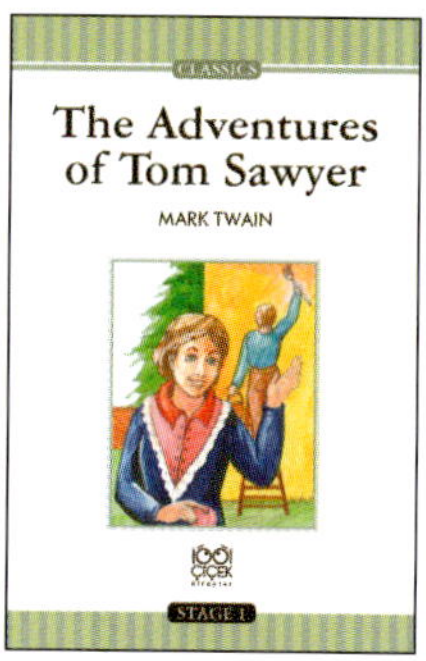

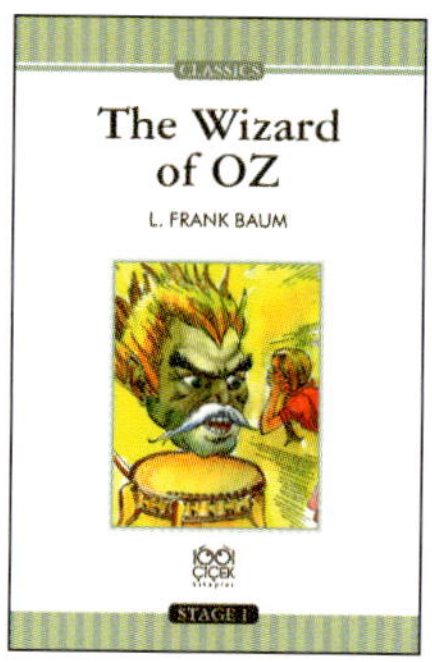

STAGE 2

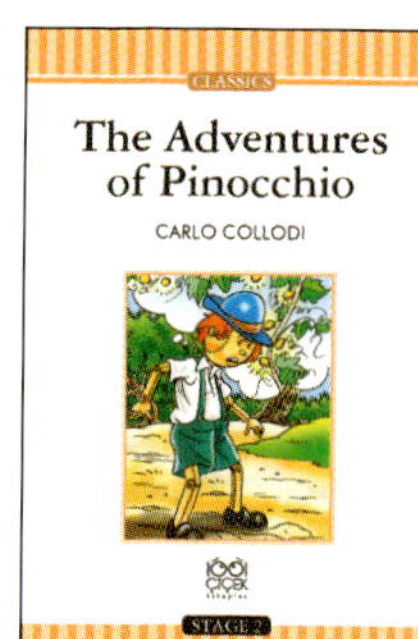

OTHER TITLES IN THE SERIES

STAGE 3

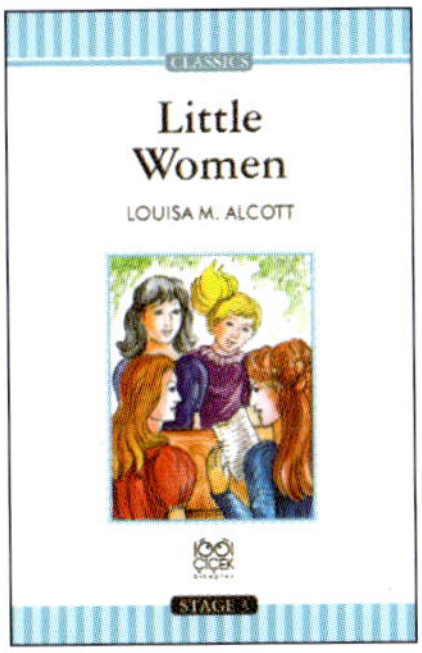

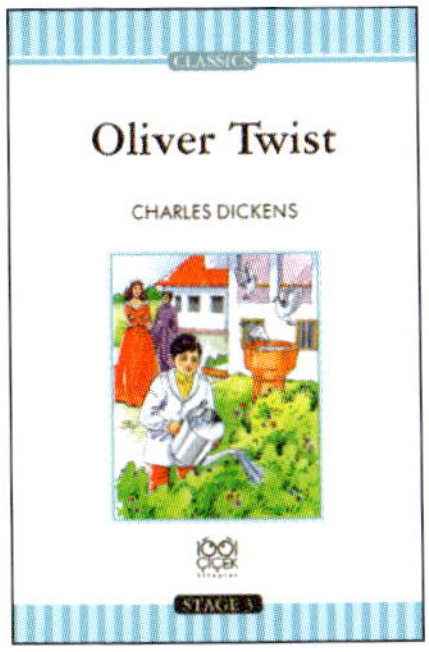

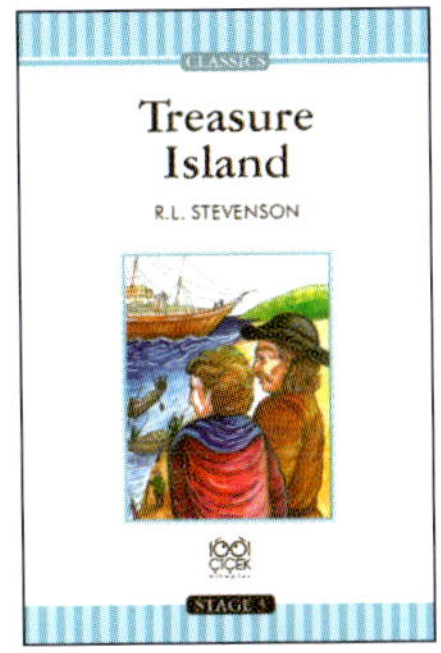

STAGE 4

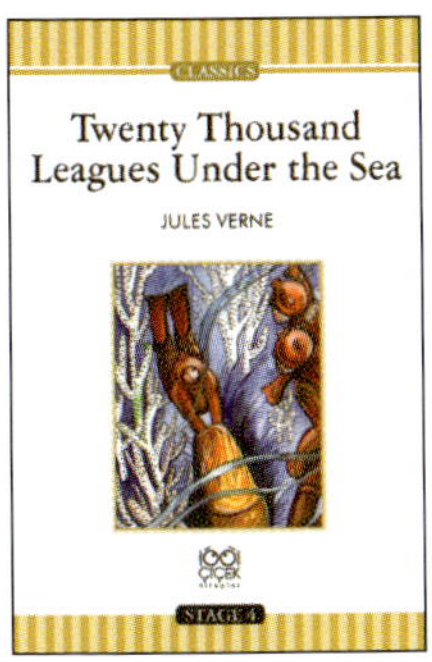

STAGE 5

STAGE 6

I l ng

Amazing Rescue Vehicles

by Frances Ridley

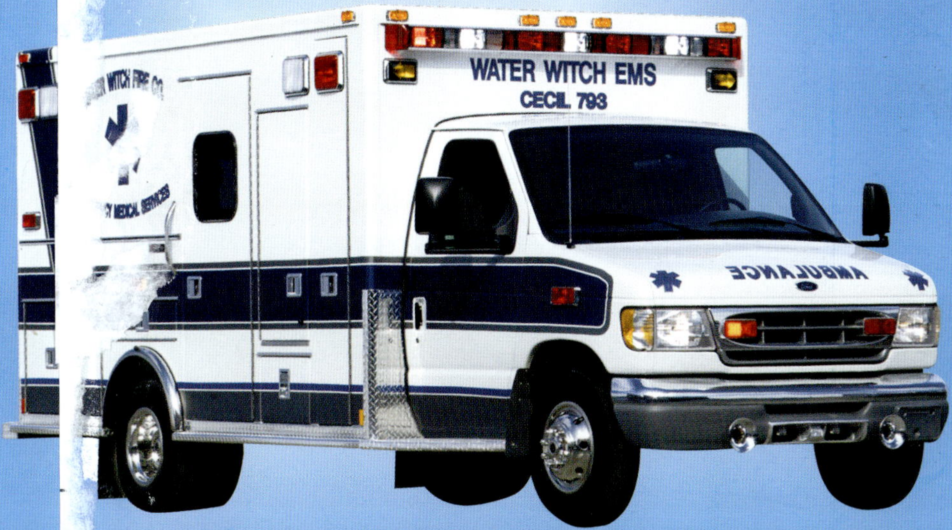

ticktock

22

Contents

Words in **bold** are explained in the glossary.

First published in Great Britain in 2008 by **ticktock Media Ltd.**,
Unit 2, Orchard Business Centre, North Farm Road,
Tunbridge Wells, Kent, TN2 3XF

We would like to thank: Penny Worms, Alix Wood and the National Literacy Trust.

ISBN 978 1 84696 775 7

Printed in China

A CIP catalogue record for this book is available from the British Library.

Picture credits: b=bottom; c=centre; t=top; r=right; l=left
Alamy: 2b, 22-23c; Bronto: 6-7c, 7tl; Check-6 Images: 12-13c, 13tl; Jane's Defence Weekly: 16-17c; Oshkosh: 2t, 4-5c, 5t, 8-9c, b/c: cr; Perry Slingsby Systems: 20-21c; Robinson Helicopters: 10-11c, 11tl; Sylvia Corday Photo Library: 21tl; US Coastguard: 14bl, 14-15c, 17tr, 18-19c, 19tr, b/c: cl

Every effort has been made to trace the copyright holders, and we apologise in advance for any unintentional omissions. We would be pleased to insert the appropriate acknowledgements in any subsequent edition of this publication.

Striker 4500

The Striker is a huge fire engine. It fights airport fires with water and foam. It holds as much water as nine normal fire engines!

The Striker has a special tool called a Snozzle™, which makes a hole in a burning plane.

It puts a camera through to see where the fire is. It can then put the fire out.

Bronto Skylift Fire Engine

The Bronto Skylift reaches higher than any other fire engine. It can reach the 33rd floor of a **skyscraper**.

Its thick hose shoots 3,800 litres of water per minute.

This Skylift can reach 72 metres in the air. It can carry people down safely.

Medtec Saturn Ambulance

Ambulances take sick people to hospital. The flashing lights warn traffic to get out of the way.

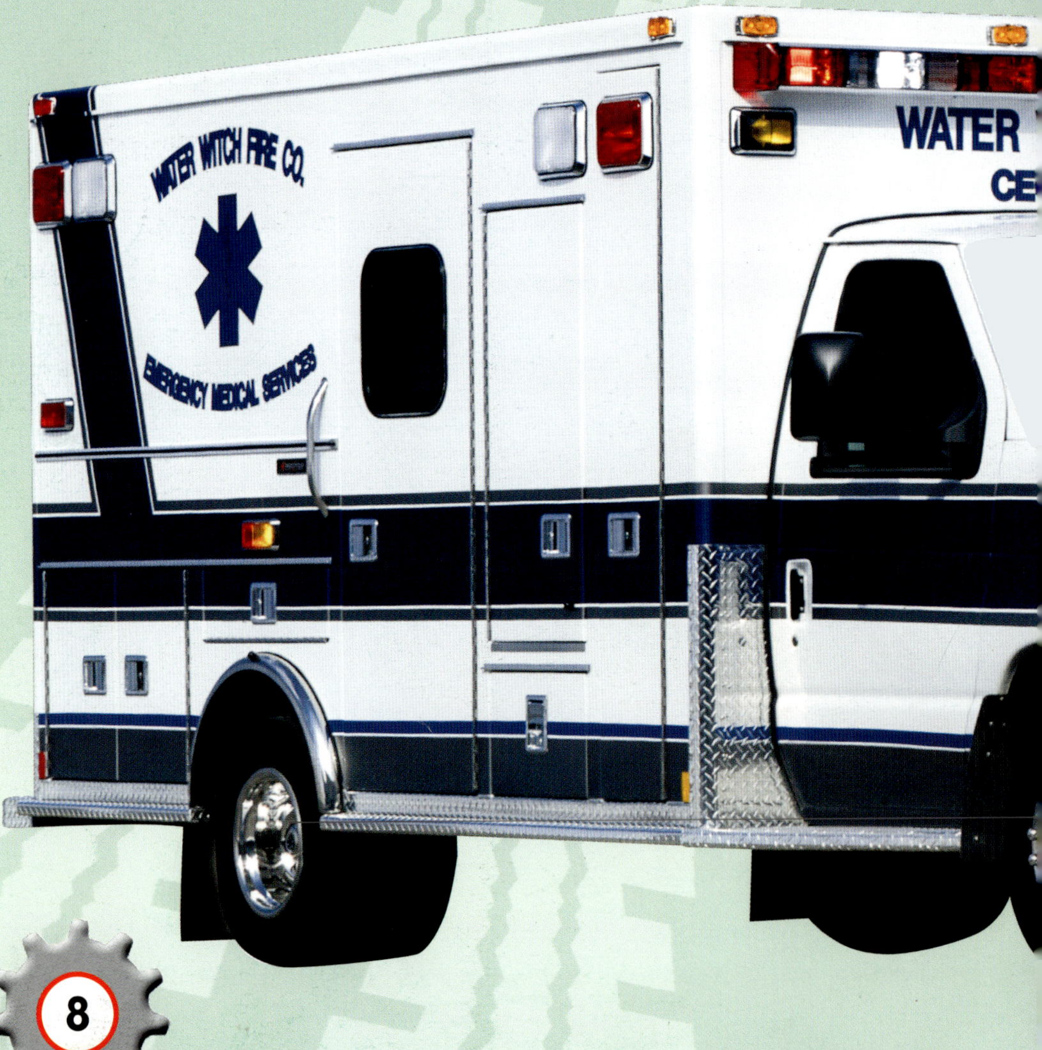

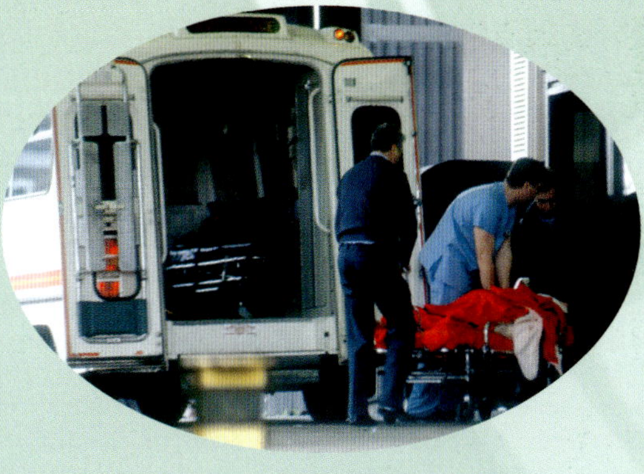

The Saturn has two back doors. There is lots of room to load stretchers on and off.

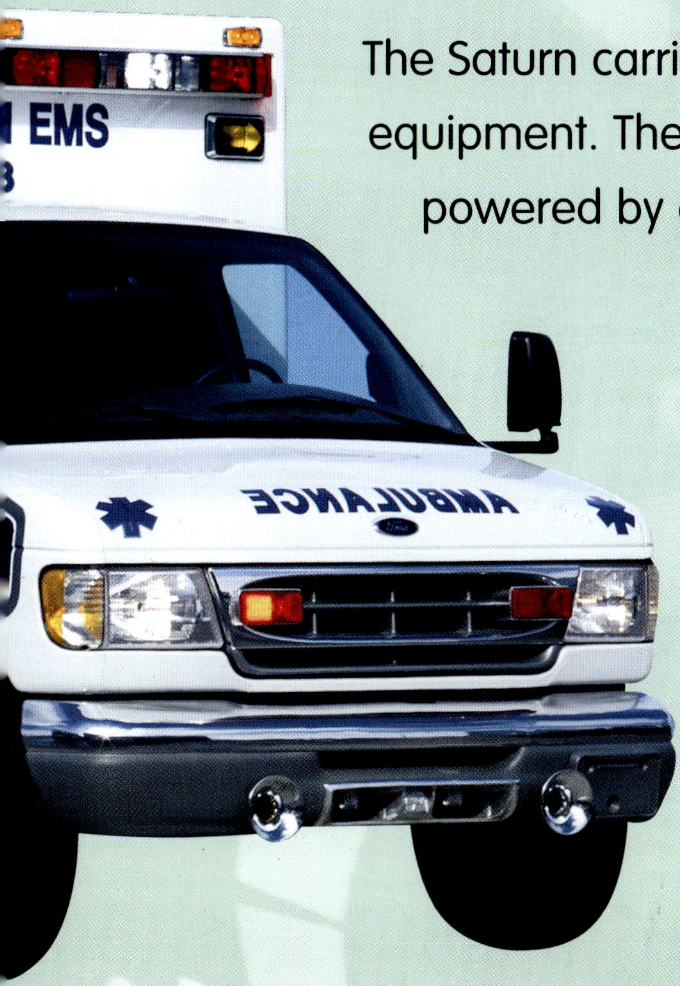

The Saturn carries life-saving equipment. The equipment is powered by a **battery pack**.

R44 Helicopter

The R44 is a police helicopter. The police can see everything that happens on the ground. They can chase criminals who try to escape.

Special equipment helps the police to do their work. The R44 has a search light, a siren and a loud speaker. It also has a **night-vision camera**.

Super Huey Helicopter

The Super Huey used to be an army helicopter. Now it fights forest fires.

It carries nine crew and their firefighting equipment.

The Super Huey can fill up its water tank from a river or lake. The water is sucked up through a hose. It can carry 916 litres of water and foam.

P-3 Orion Airtanker

The P-3 Orion Airtanker used to be a spy plane. Now, it fights forest fires. It's named after the 'Orion' group of stars.

The P-3 has a huge tank of **fire retardant** under its body. The plane drops the fire retardant in a straight line. The fire can't spread over this line.

Marine Protector

The Marine Protector is a patrol boat. It keeps the coast safe.

The Marine Protector is fast and strong. Its top speed is 45 km/h. It can go out into rough seas. It chases criminals and rescues people.

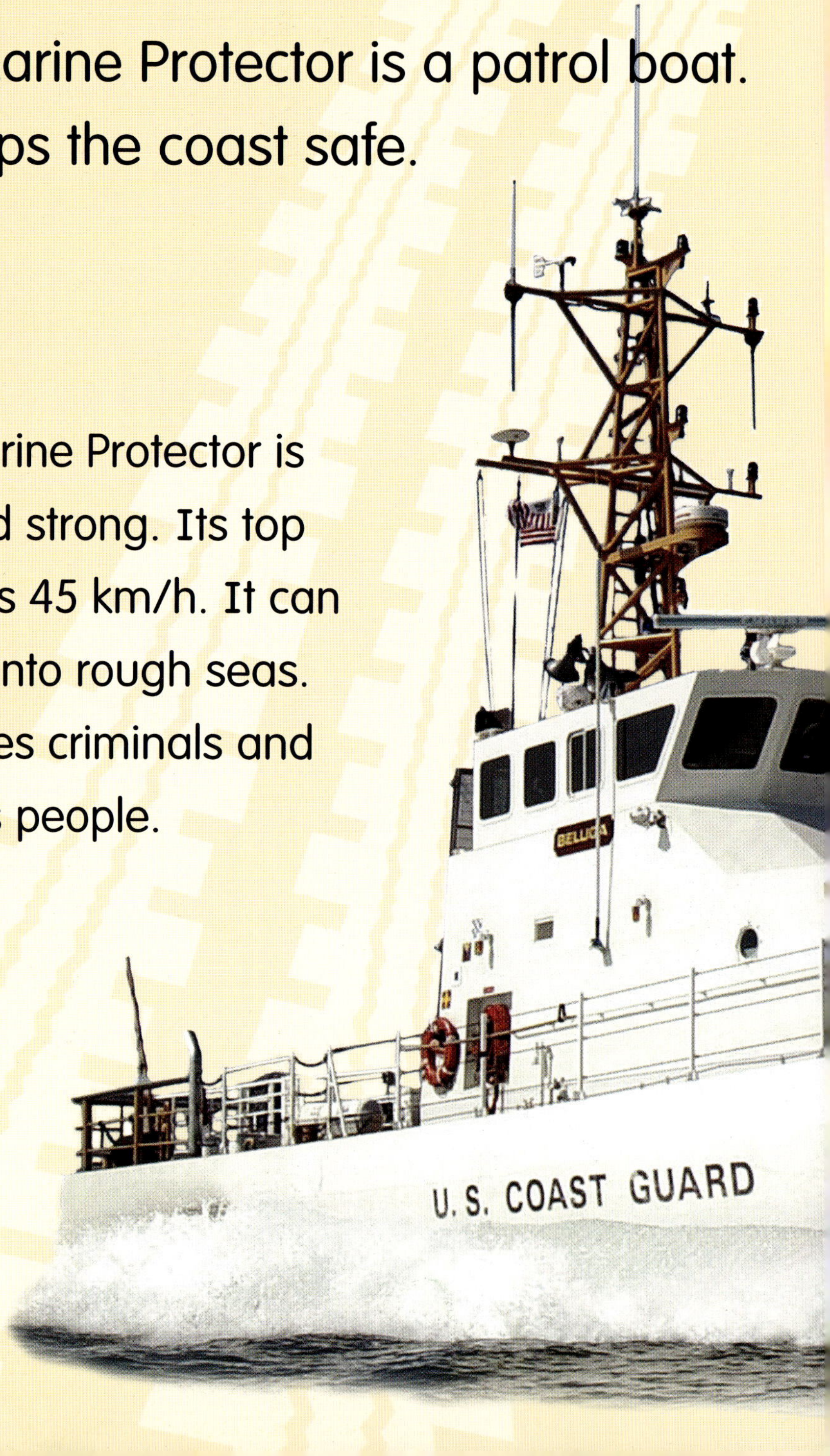

The pilot house has lots of windows so the crew can see in all directions.

HH-60J Jayhawk

The Jayhawk saves people who get into trouble at sea. It can carry four crew and six survivors. It travels at 257 km/h.

The pilot keeps the Jayhawk hovering while a rescuer is lowered down on a line. The rescuer pulls the person out of the sea. The Jayhawk pulls them both up. It takes the survivor to hospital.

LR5 and LR7 Rescue Submersibles

Rescue **submersibles** rescue people trapped in submarines.

The rescue submersible goes underwater. It finds the submarine and fixes on to it. The trapped people move into the submersible.

The LR5 has been rescuing people for over 20 years.

The LR7 was launched in 2004. It can carry 21 people.

Hagglunds BV206

The Hagglunds BV206 fights fires and rescues people. Its top speed is 51 km/h on roads and 3 km/h in the water.

It explores deserts
and jungles.
It can turn into
an ambulance.
It can even float!

The Hagglunds has
special tracks.
They can go over
snow, ice, mud,
grass or sand.

Glossary

Battery pack A supply of electricity that can be carried around.

Fire retardant A liquid or powder dropped onto fires to stop them spreading.

Night-vision camera A camera that picks up images when it is dark.

Skyscraper A very tall building.

Submersibles Boats that can go underwater.

Index